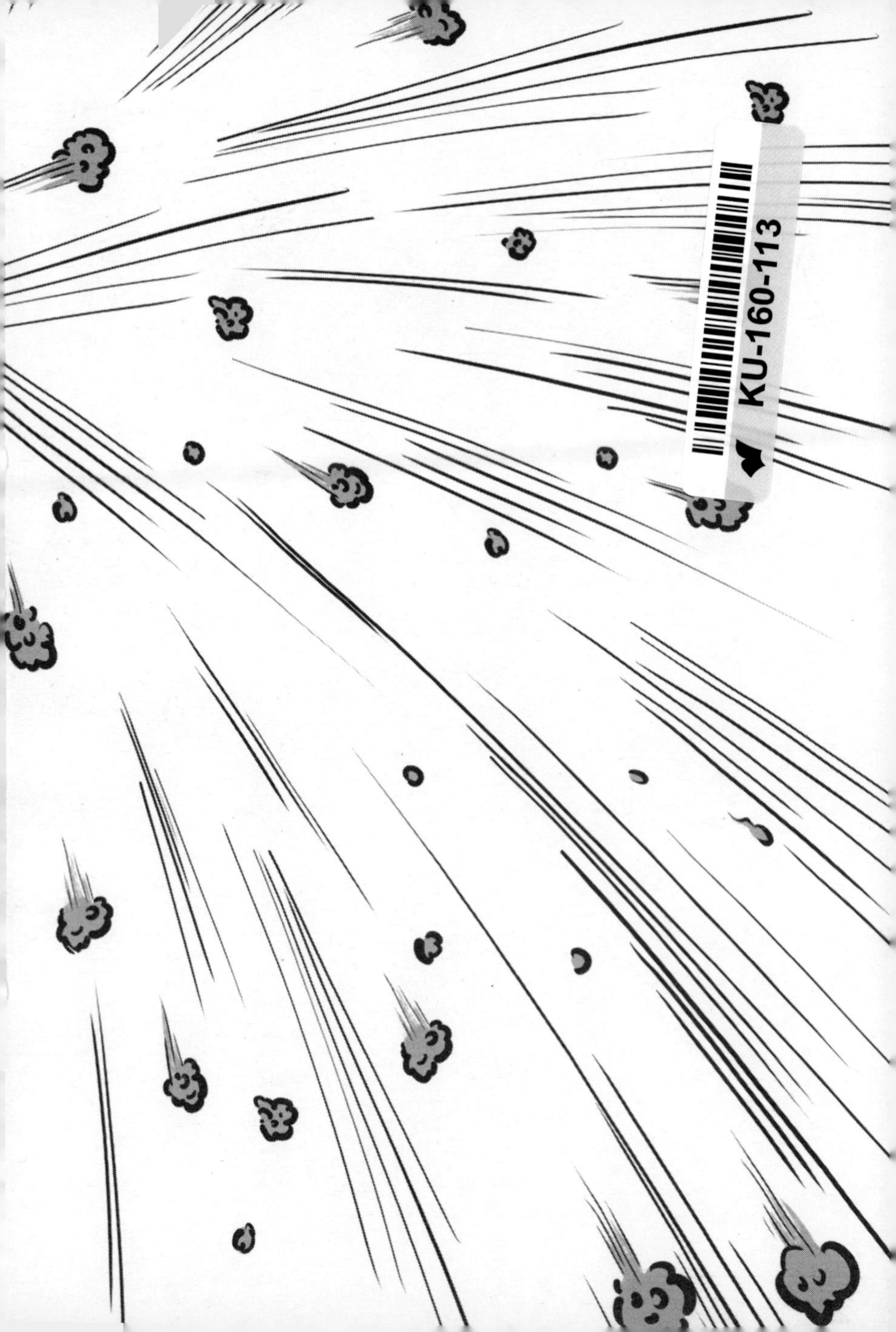
KU-160-113

ALIEN and the pants of doom

EGMONT

EGMONT

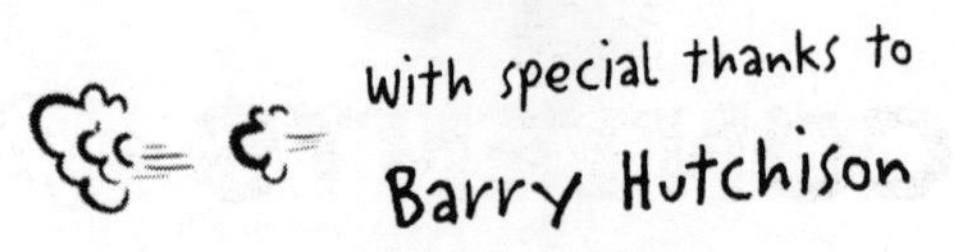

Alien and the pants of doom
First published in Great Britain 2013
by Egmont UK Limited
The Yellow Building, 1 Nicholas Road, London W11 4AN

Text copyright © 2013 Hothouse Fiction
Illustrations copyright © 2013 Chris Garbutt
All rights reserved.

The moral rights of the author and illustrator have been asserted

ISBN 978 1 4052 5507 3

1 3 5 7 9 10 8 6 4 2

www.egmont.co.uk

A CIP catalogue record for this title is available from the British Library

Printed and bound in Great Britain by CPI Group (UK) Ltd, Croydon, CR0 4YY

47424/1

All rights reserved. No part of this publication may be reproduced, stored in a retrieval system, or transmitted, in any form or by any means, electronic, mechanical, photocopying, recording or otherwise, without the prior permission of the publisher and copyright owner.

EGMONT LUCKY COIN

Our story began over a century ago, when seventeen-year-old Egmont Harald Petersen found a coin in the street.

He was on his way to buy a flyswatter, a small hand-operated printing machine that he then set up in his tiny apartment.

The coin brought him such good luck that today Egmont has offices in over 30 countries around the world. And that lucky coin is still kept at the company's head offices in Denmark.

CONTENTS

CHAPTER ONE

BREAKFAST AT THE BELLY BUSTER

A noise burst through the air like a chainsaw through a tree trunk.

DDDDNNNUUUURRRRRRRRR!

Pete Perkins opened his eyes and wiped the drool away from his chin. He was lying face down in bed, his arms spread out in a superhero flying pose.

Something's wrong, he thought sleepily. And it wasn't just the fact that it was the first day back at school after the summer holidays.

Then Pete realised. *He was lying on his belly*. He never slept on his front . . .

because usually there was a friendly green alien curled up in his belly button.

'Binko?' Pete called, turning over and prodding at his stomach frantically. His finger pushed into the warm and slightly sticky crevice of his belly button. There was nothing there – apart from some fluff and a bit of grit. He'd squashed his best friend!

'Binko!' he wailed.

'Whaaa?' came a tiny voice from over

by the bedside table.

Pete sighed with relief as he caught a glimpse of a shiny spacesuit. He moved a crusty cereal bowl and grinned when he saw the little figure snoozing behind it.

'Binko!' Pete cried. 'I thought I'd flattened you.'

The little alien yawned and gave a mini grunt. 'You nearly did. But I managed to turn my jet-pack on and fly away in time.'

'Sorry.' Pete smiled. He was happy that his friend was ok.

'And that was the loudest ickimal siren I've ever heard!' Binko gasped.

'It wasn't an ickimal siren,' Pete laughed. 'It was my alarm clock.'

Ickimals were creatures from Binko's

home planet, Pok. They were like tiny animals, only MUCH more disgusting.

A group of particularly rare ickimals had been living happily in Binko's parents' zoo on Pok, until he had accidentally let them out. The ickimals had jumped, hurged, rushed, troofed and pingled away as fast as they could on a Pokian rubbish-ship and headed straight for the smelliest, most revolting place in all the galaxy – Planet

Earth. Now they were roaming around, searching for the most gruesome grot to guzzle, and it was up to Binko and his new human friend to find them.

'There aren't any ickimals around,' Pete went on. 'But there's something even more horrible to deal with.'

'Your mum's cooking?' asked Binko.

'Worse.' Pete looked down at the crumpled uniform on his bedroom floor.

‘Summer holidays are over. It’s time to go back to school.’

‘Ooh, school!’ cried Binko. He jumped off the bedside table and began to do the Pokian foot shuffle of joy. ‘Zooper!’

‘It’s not “zooper”,’ Pete said glumly. ‘School’s boring. You have to sit still all day long and every time you try to play the tiniest trick on anyone you get told off.’

Pete dragged himself out of bed,

stretched and trudged over to where his school uniform had been lying in the same wrinkled heap for the whole summer. He gave it a quick poke with his toe to make sure his little brother Ollie hadn't hidden anything stinky underneath it, then picked it up.

'We won't even have any time to search for ickimals,' Pete said, pulling on his creased trousers.

Binko laughed. 'If school is half as disgusting as you've told me, it'll be zinging with ickimals!'

'Oh, trust me, it's . . .' Pete stopped talking as he slipped his hand into his trouser pocket. Something soft and squishy squelched between his fingers. He pulled it out to examine it.

'What is *that*?' Binko asked, looking at the lumpy grey mush in Pete's hand.

Pete gave the stuff a sniff. 'I think it's banana,' he said. He held it to his mouth and prodded it with his tongue. '**BLEURGH**.' He shuddered. 'Nope, it's pork pie. Or it was. I must have left it in there on the last day of term.'

Binko looked at him suspiciously. 'Are you sure *you're* not an ickimal?'

Pete stuffed the remains of the mouldy pork pie back in his pocket and wiped his

hand on his crumpled school shirt. 'Watch it, shorty!' He laughed and pulled the shirt on over his head.

'Sorry, big nose,' Binko replied.

'Hey! I don't have a big nose!'

'You've got a big *everything*. Big nose, big ears, big old melon head. You're flippin' *huge*.'

'Oh yeah?' Pete grinned, thinking up a really good reply. 'Well you –'

A loud shriek from through the wall made Binko jump. He fired up his jet-pack and *whooshed* into the air.

'**FLAMPERING PUFFLEFARTS!** What in the name of Garglefrunt's ear was that?' he said, gasping.

'But you *must* clean your toothy-pegs, flower petal,' called a voice from the next room. 'Who would you rather be – Mr Nice and Clean, or Mr Yucky and Smelly?'

'Sucky an' melly! Sucky an' melly!' a little voice sang out happily.

'It's only Ollie,' Pete explained, looking over at his brother's empty bed. 'He always puts up a fight when he's getting his teeth brushed. Once he flushed his toothbrush down the loo and it was blocked up for weeks. We all had to wee in a bucket until Mum could get it fixed.'

'Well done, my little munchkin,' his mum, Willow, went on, her voice getting softer as she walked down the stairs. 'Now it's time for some lovely yum-yums. Petey! Come and get your breakfast.'

Pete let Binko land on his shoulder and then climb into his hiding spot behind

Pete's ear. Then they went downstairs and slid into place at the kitchen table. Looming in front of Pete was a pint glass full of . . . *something*.

A thick, gloopy green liquid frothed over the rim of the glass and trickled down the outside. It looked like snot, only less appealing.

'Um . . . what's this?' Pete said.

Willow smiled at him encouragingly.

'It's a breakfast designed to nourish the mind, my little brainbox.' She beamed at him. 'It's Brussels sprout and turnip smoothie. With a hint of cabbage.'

'Is it supposed to be fizzing?'

Willow looked down at the glass. The foam inside it had started to bubble. 'Oh,' she frowned. 'Er . . . no.'

'Can I just have some cornflakes?' Pete asked hopefully. He looked across to where the cereal was kept.

Ollie was standing by the cupboard with a packet of rice pops in his hands, shaking it up and down. He lifted the box above his head and tipped the entire contents over himself. 'Crippy no!' he giggled. 'Crippy no!'

'What's he saying?' Binko whispered from somewhere in Pete's hair.

'Crispy snow,' replied Pete, quietly.

'Don't worry, Peteykins,' Willow cooed. 'How about I do you some lovely veggie sausages?' She skipped over to the freezer and pulled open the door. 'I'm sure I have some in –'

Dirty, smelly water sloshed out of the freezer, over Willow's bare feet and on to the kitchen floor. 'Oops,' she said. 'What could have happened?'

'Um . . . I think the freezer's broken,'

Pete told her, matter-of-factly.

Willow looked down at the puddle, which had half-thawed lumps of mouldy vegetables floating in it. She looked up at Ollie, and the mountain of cereal building up on top of his head. Then she looked back at the rotting carrots and broccoli squelching between her toes.

'On second thoughts . . .' she said. 'Why don't we go to a café?'

'Hey, look, there's G-Bob,' said Pete, pointing across the café to a corner booth. His grandfather sat hunched over a table, cramming food into his mouth.

'Oh, lovely!' Willow exclaimed. 'We can have a real family breakfast! Yoohoo, Dad! We'll come and join you!'

G-Bob looked up and groaned, then tried to hide behind the spatter-marked menu. As Willow slid into the booth and sat next to him, G-Bob grunted and shovelled mouthfuls in even faster than before.

'This place is *disgusting*,' Binko whispered, scanning the room with a tiny machine covered with flashing buttons. It whizzed and beeped faster and faster as Binko pointed it around. 'Bugs and germs everywhere. The Filth-o-Meter's off the chart. It's perfect ickimal territory. Be on the lookout.'

Pete nodded and slipped into the booth opposite G-Bob. His grandad was wearing a grubby vest and worn trousers that were held up by string, and his feet were strapped into open-toed sandals, showing off his thick yellow toenails. Rivers of grease were flowing down the sides of his mouth into the wiry hairs of his long matted beard. Pete was impressed – G-Bob didn't normally look so smart.

'What you want?' snarled a voice suddenly. Pete looked up at Big Len, the owner of the Belly Buster Café. He stood by the table, a notepad in his hand and a scowl on his face.

'What do you have?' Willow asked.

'Sausage, egg and beans,' Big Len replied.

'Is there a vegetarian option?' Willow asked, hopefully.

mum

MENU

'Yeah. Egg and beans. You'll all be having that, anyway,' he told them. 'No sausages left.'

'How could you run out of sausages?' Pete gasped. He glanced across at G-Bob's plate. It was piled high with crusty brown sausages, all gently steaming.

'Hands off,' G-Bob warned, shoving another banger into his mouth and letting a new wave of fat trickle down his big, bushy beard. 'I've counted 'em all.'

Pete's belly rumbled loudly. Binko's belly rumbled too, only not so noisily. They had to get some of those sausages, no matter what!

CHAPTER TWO

SPICY SAUSAGE SURPRISE

'Mmmm, *tasty*,' G-Bob said, spraying bits of sausage across the table and grinning messily at Pete. 'This is even better than that cheese I made in me shed.'

Pete tried not to laugh as he thought

about the first ickimal he and Binko had caught – the hairy, ape-like, cheese-loving chimple that they had secretly plopped in G-Bob's cheese cauldron for safe keeping.

'Have you stopped making cheese then?' Pete asked, wondering what weird hobby G-Bob had taken up this week.

'Yeah, now I've started beef bowling instead,' his grandpa said. 'You get corned beef an' make it into a big ball . . .' G-Bob leaned forwards, trailing his beard over his plate. 'No funny stuff with beef bowling. There's somethin' very *strange* about that cheese.' G-Bob sat back in his seat and used his fork to scratch under his armpit. 'It's almost like it's *alive* . . .'

'You lot ordering something or not?' growled Big Len.

'Three egg and beans, please,' said Willow.

'Trees, egg and beems!' Ollie yelled. He thumped the table with a pudgy little fist, catching the edge of his spoon.

The spoon went spinning up, through the air . . .

. . . and smacked Big Len's head with a

THUNK.

'Again, again,' Ollie laughed. Then he blew a raspberry at the café owner.

'Bleeeurgh!' Big Len stomped off across the café towards the swing door that led to the kitchen.

'I know how we're going to get a sausage,' Pete whispered, as quietly as he could.

'Steal one?' Binko guessed.

'G-Bob's counted them, remember? We can't just steal one, we need to *swap* one.'

'We haven't got anything to swap with,' Binko replied.

'You're going to sneak to the kitchen

and bring something back,' Pete said.

'Like what?'

'I don't know. Something sausage-shaped. But you can't let anyone see you.'

Binko looked around the café. There were a few other people about, spread across the room. 'Could be tricky,' he said.

'I have an idea.' Pete pretended to scratch his ear and scooped Binko into his hand. With his other hand he pulled the mouldy mush from his pocket. Out of sight beneath the table, he squidged the furry grey gloop of the mouldy pork pie down over Binko's head.

'You can pretend you're a mouse,' Pete whispered. 'There's bound to be a whole load of them round here. You'll fit in perfectly.'

'Ooh, this is like a Mucklovian mud bath,' said Binko. 'Lovely.'

With that, the little alien scampered down Pete's leg and off towards the kitchen.

'Looking forward to your first day back at school, fluffle-cake?' Willow asked.

'Oh, can't wait,' Pete replied. 'I mean, who doesn't love maths?'

'D'you know what I love?' slurped G-Bob.

'Beards?' guessed Pete.

'Body odour?' guessed Willow.

'Poopity pants!' shouted Ollie, getting into the spirit of things.

'Sausages.' G-Bob grinned, showing his brown and yellow teeth. 'I *love* these sausages. All meaty an' greasy an' tasty an' that. Shame you ain't havin' none.'

We'll see about that! thought Pete.

A scream from across the room made him jump. He looked round to see half of the café's customers leaping to their feet. They pointed at the ground, their faces white with shock. 'Mouse!' one woman cried. 'M-M-M-MOUSE!'

Pete felt a tickle on his leg as Binko returned. 'Mission accomplished!' the little alien declared proudly.

'Binko,' sighed Pete under his breath. 'You were supposed to try and stay out of sight . . .'

'I did,' Binko replied. 'That's a *real* mouse.'

The café was in chaos now. The room

was filled with screams and shrieks as people spotted the mouse. Then there were clangs and crashes as they dropped their cutlery and ran out the door.

'FLAMPERING PUFFLEFARTS!'

Binko gasped. 'The mouse must be a fearsome animal. I didn't know humans could run that fast!'

'Oh yeah,' Pete sniggered. 'They're *terrifying*! They've got huge teeth and they eat people whole. Anyway, did you get something to swap?'

'Of course!' Binko said, looking round nervously for mice. 'It's under your chair.'

Pete looked down. Right by his shoe lay a chilli pepper. It was vaguely the same size as a sausage, and sort of a similar shape. But the colour . . .

'It's bright red,' Pete muttered.

'It was all I could get.' Binko shrugged. 'Apart from eggs and beans, that is. And they aren't going to work . . .'

'Hmmmm,' Pete looked at the chilli thoughtfully. 'We'll have to disguise it.'

Binko paused. 'Well, I could probably find a false moustache . . .'

'Not like that,' Pete whispered, looking around. Ollie was blasting streams of ketchup and brown sauce across the table. That gave Pete an idea.

'All we have to do is distract G-Bob long enough to make the swap,' Pete whispered. No answer came. 'Binko?'

Pete saw a flash of mouldy grey darting towards his mum's feet. A nearby scream almost made his eardrums pop. Willow had leaped up on to her chair and was staring down at the floor. 'Mouse! I saw the mouse!'

'*Flippin' 'eck*, sit down, woman!' G-Bob barked, looking up from his plate.

Nice one, Binko! thought Pete. He quickly pried the brown sauce away from Ollie and gave him Willow's purse to decorate with ketchup. Then he scooped up the chilli and squeezed the whole bottle over it, until it was completely covered in gooey brown gunk. Pete glanced up, but Willow was still waving her arms about wildly. G-Bob was staring at her with his mouth open so wide that some half-chewed food had fallen out into his beard.

Pete studied the chilli. It still didn't look *much* like a sausage, but then G-Bob never paid attention to what he was eating anyway, he just stuffed it into his gaping mouth.

With a lightning-fast flick of his wrist, Pete switched the chilli with a sausage from G-Bob's gigantic pile.

Just then Len arrived, carrying three plates heaped messily with beans and fried eggs. He slapped them on the table, then stomped off back to the kitchen. Pete slipped the stolen sausage on to his plate. 'Len must have found one after all,' he said as innocently as he could.

G-Bob eyed him suspiciously, then looked down at his breakfast. He counted his sausages. Then he counted on his fingers. Then he counted his sausages again, more slowly this time. He narrowed his eyes at Pete once more and grunted.

Pete felt a movement next to his ear, and knew that Binko was back.

No longer able to see the 'mouse', Willow slowly lowered herself into her seat. Across the table, G-Bob's fork speared the sauce-coated chilli pepper.

It was halfway to the old man's mouth when Pete remembered something. 'Wait,' he whispered to Binko. 'Aren't chilli peppers supposed to be spicy?'

'Oh yes,' Binko said. 'There's one on Pok that sets fire to your tongue and makes smoke come out your bottom.'

Pete turned to his grandad, but G-Bob's yellow gnashers were already closing down on the sauce-coated chilli.

Pete shrugged and settled back in his chair. If it *was* hot then this would be worth watching!

G-Bob chewed once and his mouth dropped open. Then his eyes grew wide and panicky.

'YEEEEEEOW!'

G-Bob howled, spitting bits of chilli and sauce everywhere. 'Hot, hot, HOT!'

He made a strangled gargling noise as he clutched at his throat and flapped his hands in front of his mouth.

'Hoo hoo ha ha!' he cried.

Ollie clapped his pudgy hands together. 'Funny monkey,' he gurgled happily.

G-Bob looked down at his baby grandson and spotted a bottle in his hands. He lunged, grabbed it, and tore open the lid. In one big gulp, G-Bob emptied the entire contents of the bottle down his throat.

'**FLAMPERING PUFFLEFARTS!**'

Binko said in Pete's ear. 'That was amazing. I didn't know humans could blow steam out of their ears!'

'It's not over yet . . .' Pete mumbled,

watching as G-Bob's cheeks bulged.

With a twirl that a ballerina would have been proud of, G-Bob twisted around and spat out a mouthful of the brown liquid over the people eating at the next table.

'*Vinegar!*' he spluttered, reading the bottle's label. His cheeks pulled in and his lips pursed into a tight circle as the bitterness of the vinegar tingled on his tonsils. '**Euuuuuuurrrggghhhh!**'

G-Bob leaped up, barged through the café door and ran out on to the pavement. His screaming continued all the way to the bottom of the road, where he could just be seen with his head dunked in the village bird bath.

'Oh, well,' Pete chuckled, picking up his grandad's plate. 'Looks like G-Bob doesn't want his sausages after all.'

CHAPTER THREE
FART-TASTIC!

Pete's happiness didn't last long. He'd barely taken one bite of sausage when a familiar face poked up from the next table. Pete's heart sank. 'Oh no,' he muttered.

'Who's that?' Binko asked.

'That's Billy,' Pete whispered. 'The meanest boy in my class. I was so busy with the sausage plan I didn't see him before. No wonder his family are the only ones who haven't run away from the mouse. They probably eat mice for breakfast – raw.'

'I'll get you for this, Perkins,' Billy scowled, wiping away the vinegar that dripped from his face.

Willow stopped picking beans out of Ollie's hair and smiled at Pete distractedly. 'Oh, has G-Bob gone already?' she asked. 'I was going to get him to drop you off at the school gate. Never mind, maybe you could go with your little friend here?' Behind Willow's back, Billy pulled a face at Pete.

'Oh no . . . um,' Pete muttered, trying desperately to think of a reason why he couldn't go with Billy, who was now pulling the corners of his mouth wider and turning his eyelids inside out. If there were such a thing as face-pulling olympics, Billy would win a gold medal.

Willow was still smiling at Pete. Any minute now she'd make them walk together. The journey was long enough for Billy to steal his lunch money, beat him up and give him a wedgie, all before school even started. Pete gulped loudly. 'Binko, I need another distraction,' he muttered.

Suddenly a high-pitched alarm began to sound in his ear.

'OW!' Pete cried.

'Are you ok, fluffle-puffle?' Willow asked.

'Sorry, Pete, ickimal alert!' Binko whispered, stopping the noise before anyone else could hear it. 'Doesn't matter though, Billy's leaving.'

With a final tongue-out, eye-roll combination, Billy turned and left. The stink hit them a second later, like a frying pan to the face. It almost knocked Pete off his chair.

It smelled like rotten eggs and dog poo . . . only worse. It was a stink so powerful that Pete couldn't just *smell* it, he could *taste* it. Up until that moment, the worst stench he'd ever come across had been from one of G-Bob's dirty socks. Now, that record had been broken.

'What *is* that?' Pete asked, holding his nose and trying not to breathe.

'I don't know,' Binko said in his ear.

'But a disgusting pong like that is definitely the work of an ickimal . . .' Binko started pressing buttons on the arm of his spacesuit. 'And it looks like it's hiding near Billy!'

Pete groaned. 'Actually, Mum, I *will* walk to school with Billy,' he said quickly.

'All right, my clever little chipmunk,' Willow said, as Pete started stuffing the rest of G-Bob's sausages into his pockets.'And remember, learning can be fun, if you just open your mind . . .' Willow raised her arms above her head and closed her eyes.

'Yes . . . OK . . . got to go!' Pete looked out the window, where Billy's family were already disappearing down the street.

'Oh. Yes. Sorry,' said Willow. She lowered her arms. 'Well, tatty bye, sweet pea! Have a great day.'

'Baa-baa, Pit,' said Ollie, waving cheerfully with both pudgy hands.

'Bye-bye, Ollie,' Pete replied, waving back. With Binko nestled in his hair, Pete rushed out of the café.

'Billy's always farting,' Pete told Binko as they followed him at a safe distance. 'He makes people smell his bum burps when they won't give him their lunch money. They aren't normally as bad as that though.'

Binko thought for a moment. 'Ickimal

close by . . . boy with a bad case of trouser trumps . . . hmmm. It can only mean one thing. We have a pantpiper on the loose! We'll have to stay close to Billy so I can track it down.'

Pete stuffed his fingers up his nose to block the smell. 'OK, let's do it,' he said.

It was going to be a long, stinky day.

Pete followed Billy through the gates of Little Retching Primary and into the crumbling old building, the smell from Billy's bottom wafting all around him. When Billy sat down in class, Pete made sure that he sat at the desk behind him – right in the firing line.

Pete's teacher Miss Penicketty stepped into the classroom a second after him. 'Sit down, children, sit down,' she said in a firm voice.

Pete dropped his school books on the desk in front of him, then ducked down to talk to Binko. 'Right, then, what's a pantpiper?' he whispered.

Before Binko could reply, a loud noise shook the classroom.

PAAAAAAAAAARP!

Pete giggled. 'That sounded like a massive –'

THHHUUURRPAAARP!

The sound came again.

'Ugh, that *stinks*,' complained a girl just a few rows in front of Pete. 'Who's doing that?'

FAAAAAAA AAAART!

'THAT'S ENOUGH!' shrieked Miss Penicketty, clamping a hankie to her face. 'Whoever is making those disgusting sounds, stop it at once!' Suddenly she staggered back in horror as the full force of the aroma caught in her throat. 'Oh, my,' she muttered. 'That's . . . that's . . . powerful.'

'She looks like she's going to faint,' whispered Binko.

'Call an ambulance,' replied Pete with a smirk.

'Get a zongledook,' yelped Binko.

'And a gas mask,' sniggered Pete.

'Pass her a flarf!' They both laughed.

Miss Penicketty had been Pete's teacher since reception, and Pete had seen her clean up a lot of disgusting things.

He'd watched her mop up Roger Murphy's wee, Lisa Wilson's sick and an anonymous poo that had once appeared on the classroom floor. Miss Penicketty had a stomach of steel. But Pete had to admit, even *she* looked like she was struggling with this smell.

PRRRRRRRUUUURRP!

In the row in front of Pete, Billy shifted uncomfortably in his seat. Although his eyes were watering, Pete kept a lookout for any sign of an ickimal.

There was silence for a few seconds, and then:

PRURP-PRRRRRUP!

The force of the blast lifted Billy several centimetres off his seat! He grabbed for the desk, pulling himself back down before Miss Penicketty spotted him.

Kids started rushing to open the classroom windows and gulp in mouthfuls of fresh air, some using their maths books to try to waft the stench outside.

'Stop it!' yelped Miss Penicketty. 'Stop it right now!'

'Is it the pantpiper?' Pete whispered as he stuffed a yellow crayon up his right nostril and a rubber up his left.

'Yes,' Binko explained. 'A pantpiper

is an ickimal with a taste for the smelly. It likes the worst, most disgusting stinks around. And its favourite feast is to gobble up another creature's loud-clouds.'

Pete gasped. 'You don't mean . . .'

Binko nodded. 'Fluffs, bottom rumbles, pop-offs, stink wind. It snorts them in through its snout and lets them brew and bubble around in its belly for a while,' he explained. 'Then, when it's good and ready, it releases them.'

'Releases them?' asked Pete.

'In a series of stink explosions ten times worse than the original smell! It's a bottom-boom booster. A bum-gas blaster. A parp projector. When its victim lets a honker slip out, the pantpiper hoovers it up, then does ten extra-stinky long-lasting trumps in its place! It's an *amplifier*,' Binko said. 'For *farts*!'

Pete looked back at Billy, who was wriggling in his seat. 'So now it's . . .'

'Yep.' Binko nodded. 'The pantpiper is hiding in Billy's briefs!'

CHAPTER FOUR

BLOWING IN THE WIND

It didn't take long for Binko to be proved right. Ten seconds – and a thunderous bum-wobbler – later, two wide round eyes on long slug-like stalks popped up above the waistband of Billy's trousers, followed by a big snuffling snout. The pantpiper turned its gaze towards Binko and then, with a squeak of alarm, it ducked back down out of sight.

Binko moved quickly. He dropped from Pete's ear to the desk and snatched a broken pencil stub from Pete's pencil case. The stub was bigger than Binko, and he carried it above his head like a pole vaulter.

'I'm going in!' he cried, in a voice just

loud enough for Pete to hear. Then he ran towards the edge of the desk, dug the pencil stub deep into the wood and made a spectacular vault over to Billy.

Up, up, up

he went in a graceful arc before plunging down, down and vanishing into the back of Billy's trousers.

The bully gave a yelp. Miss Penicketty looked at him and finally noticed his wide eyes and pale face.

'Are you all right, Billy?' she asked.

'*Eeep*,' squeaked Billy, nodding his head. 'F-fine thanks.'

Miss Penicketty turned to the blackboard, but Pete kept watching the back of Billy's trousers, which were jumping about as Binko and the pantpiper battled beneath them.

'AWOoooOeeeeeughm!' Billy whimpered, clutching the edges of the desk tightly. 'Eeeee-OOOo-cha-um!'

'Sorry, Billy? Did you say something?' Miss Penicketty asked.

'N-no, Miss,' Billy replied. 'Not – OoooWWWWeeee – not m-me.'

Miss Penicketty looked at him for a long time. 'Right, that's enough silliness,' she said firmly. 'Time for some lovely maths equations.'

She turned back to the blackboard just as a movement by Billy's belt caught Pete's eye. The pantpiper had popped up again. Pete saw his chance.

Diving over the desk, Pete grabbed for the ickimal. He felt his fingers catch on to something, and pulled as hard as he could.

'YeeeeeeeOW!' howled Billy.

Pete had missed the pantpiper and hooked Billy's pants instead, yanking them up sharply and giving him a killer wedgie.

Billy span round, furious, and Pete leaped back. 'Sorry!' he gulped. 'I was just . . . I didn't mean to . . .'

But Billy wasn't listening. He threw himself at Pete and they both crashed to the floor.

'Get off!' Pete cried, trying to twist free.

PAAAAAAAARP!

Another boom exploded from Billy's

bottom. It was so powerful it sent them rolling across the classroom, bumping into desks and chairs along the way.

'What's going on?' demanded Miss Penicketty. 'Stop that!'

PAAAAAAARP!

One more stinker erupted from Billy's backside. It propelled them back the way they'd come. As they struggled, Pete spotted Binko hopping out from Billy's waistband and racing up the bully's back. With a heroic leap, the little alien landed in Pete's hair, just as Miss Penicketty caught Billy by the shirt and yanked him to his feet.

'Right, that is *quite enough*,' the teacher snapped. All at once the stench from the pantpiper's amplified farts hit her, and for a moment Pete thought she was going to be sick on Billy's head. She mopped her forehead with her hankie and spoke in a quavery voice. 'I will not tolerate fighting in my class,' she said, holding her nose. 'Both of you, go to Mrs Brimwell's office.'

Pete stood up. 'But –'

Miss Penicketty's face went an angry shade of red. 'The headmistress's office,' she repeated. '*Right now!*'

Pete sat in the corridor outside Mrs Brimwell's office, waiting to be called in. Billy sat directly across from him. His whole body was trembling. He looked terrified, but Pete knew Billy wasn't afraid of the head teacher. Over the years, Billy had probably spent more time in her office than Mrs Brimwell had. He was no stranger to getting in trouble, and he'd never looked worried about it before. It had to be the pantpiper that was making him so nervous.

Sure enough, Billy was sitting on his hands, holding his buttocks closed, trying to stop more of the toxic gas leaking out.

'It's the big one,' said Binko.

'What?' whispered Pete.

'The pantpiper,' Binko explained. 'It's bigger than a gnarlock, and fiercer than a gnarlock's mum. I recognise it from the zoo. It was the most vicious pantpiper we've ever had on Pok.'

'Before you let them all escape,' Pete teased.

'Do you have to keep reminding me?' asked Binko, glumly.

'Yep,' said Pete, smiling. 'But look on the bright side – we'd never have had all this fun if you hadn't.'

Binko's face brightened. 'Doesn't look like Billy's enjoying himself much,' the little alien said.

Pete looked across at Billy. He was bouncing up and down in his seat and biting his lip. His face was turning a worrying shade of red.

'We'd better think of a way to get the pantpiper back, then.'

'It won't be easy,' Binko said. 'A direct hit from a piper's pumper could knock you out for a week!'

Pete thought about this for a moment. 'Ouch.'

'Exactly. We'll have to be sneakier than a blooglesnuck if we're going to catch him.'

Across the corridor, Billy gave a loud whimper. His face was scrunched up like a baby about to cry, and his fists were clenched tight. Pete and Binko edged away.

'He's holding one in,' Binko whispered.

'He needs to let rip with a bum-blast of his own, but he's keeping it in because he's scared it'll be like the others.'

'Of course! He doesn't know about the pantpiper,' whispered Pete. 'He thinks *he's* been doing those mega-farts.'

'Exactly. Only problem is, the longer he brews it, the worse it's going to be when it escapes. And if you think *his* bum blast is bad . . .'

‘The pantpiper’s will be ten times worse!’ Pete realised.

Billy was trembling all over as he tried not to trump.

Just then the door to the head’s office was thrown open and Mrs Brimwell appeared. ‘Right boys, in you come,’ she said, beckoning for them to enter.

Pete stood up and walked quickly into the room. Behind him, Billy eased

himself to his feet without bending his legs. He began to waddle slowly towards the open office door.

'Walk properly, Billy,' Mrs Brimwell commanded. Billy gave her a look of panic and shuffled a bit faster, until he was standing beside the desk in the head teacher's room.

'Sit down, both of you,' Mrs Brimwell said seriously, as she closed the door and

smoothed her hair neatly behind her ears.

She moved round to the other side of the desk and sat down, peering at them over her glasses. Pete took a seat. Billy didn't move. 'C-can I s-stay standing?' he asked. His voice was shaking as badly as the rest of him.

'Uh-oh. This doesn't look good for Billy,' Binko said stifling a giggle.

'You mean "*May* I stay standing?",' Mrs Brimwell corrected. 'And no, you may not. Sit.'

With a groan, Billy gradually began to lower himself down on to the chair. His bum stayed silent.

'I'm very disappointed,' Mrs Brimwell told them. 'In both of you. Fighting in class is not acceptable. You both need to . . . to . . .' Her voice trailed off as her gaze rested on Billy's bulging eyes. 'Are you all right, Billy?'

Billy forced a grin and quickly nodded. His face had gone the same colour as the chilli Binko had borrowed from Big Len's kitchen. Sweat dripped down his

forehead like raindrops.

As he sat rocking gently from bum cheek to bum cheek, Mrs Brimwell watched him, puzzled. 'Billy, what *are* you doing . . .'

Letting out a small squeak, Billy suddenly stood up. His whole body went stiff and his eyes became two giant saucers. A shudder passed through him from his head to his toes, and a faint whimper escaped his lips.

'Look out!' Binko warned, diving for cover behind Pete's ear. 'Billy's going to blow!'

CHAPTER FIVE
LETTING IT OUT

'Look at his face!' Binko said.

Pete watched Billy's mouth pull into a scowl. His eyes were clamped shut, his teeth bared. His forehead was more creased than Pete's school-shirt when he'd screwed it up to use it as a football.

And then, suddenly, Billy relaxed. The panic vanished from his face, and was replaced by a look of relief.

'What just happened?' Pete said.

'I think Billy just launched a silent-but-deadly backside-bazooka,' Binko explained, shaking his head sadly. 'He just couldn't hold it in any longer.'

Pete gasped. 'But the pantpiper!'

'. . . will be hoovering it up.' Binko nodded. 'Billy's trouser trumpet will be bubbling and brewing in its belly.'

'What should we do?' Pete asked.

'Run for our lives?' suggested Binko.

Mrs Brimwell pushed past Pete, making for a cupboard directly behind Billy. She waved her hand in front of her face. 'I think we need some air freshener in here,' she mumbled. She bent down to open the cupboard, bringing her head directly in line with Billy's bum.

Pete realised what was going to happen next seconds before it did . . .

PAAAAAAAAARPPPPP!

A sound like booming thunder shook the room. The blast from Billy's pants hit Mrs Brimwell's face like a hundred-mile-an-hour gale.

Her glasses flew across the room and her hair stood on end with the force of the impact. She staggered backwards, coughing and spluttering, and stumbled into her chair.

For a few seconds she just sat there, clutching the chair tightly. Her breath wheezed in and out. Her face was the colour of pea soup and her eyes looked watery and bloodshot.

'B-Billy,' she croaked, struggling for air, 'I think you should go and see the n-nurse.'

Billy nodded and hurried out of the office. 'And y-you can go back to class, Pete,' the head added. 'Just don't do . . . whatever it is you did again.'

'Yes, Miss. Thanks, Miss,' Pete said, before rushing out.

Pete could hear Binko giggling as

they made their way down the corridor. '**FLAMPERING PUFFLEFARTS**, that was brilliant!' the little alien gasped. 'Did you see her face!'

Pete laughed, but it turned into a gurgle as Billy grabbed him by the shirt and slammed him up against the wall.

'You'd better not tell anyone about what happened in there,' the bully growled. 'If I find out you've told even *one person*,

I'll give you a knuckle sandwich. Get it?'

Pete nodded. 'Got it.'

'Good,' Billy said. He released his grip on Pete's shirt, then walked off along the corridor. The bully's cocky swagger was back.

'That was nice of him,' said Binko.

Pete frowned. 'What? No it wasn't!'

'Yes it was. He offered to make you a sandwich. Very generous of him.'

'No, Binko, a *knuckle* sandwich isn't actually a sandwich. It's a punch. He was saying he'd punch me.'

'By the three bellies of Zingler, you humans have some strange sayings,' Binko replied.

'Billy seems back to normal, anyway,' Pete said glumly. 'Does that mean the pantpiper's gone?'

Binko shook his head. 'They don't

just leave. They'll only move on if they've found somewhere even smellier to snuffle around.'

'But where could it –?'

PAAAAAAAAAARP!

'Oh my,' yelped Mrs Brimwell from inside her office. 'Pardon *me*!'

Pete and Binko stood completely still, then exploded with laughter.

'Shhhhh!' Pete gasped as he moved away from the headmistress's door. 'She'll hear!'

'Mrs Brimwell!' Binko giggled. 'The pantpiper's jumped over to Mrs Brimwell!'

From inside, they heard the sound of several more loud trumps.

'*Pardon me!*' Binko said in a high girly voice, making Pete start laughing again. He giggled until his stomach hurt.

Binko laughed so much he fell off Pete's ear and had to turn his jet pack on to stop him hitting the floor.

'She must be smellier than she looks,' Binko snorted. 'She must brew up some real honkers for the pantpiper to pick her over Billy.'

'How are we going to get it back now?' Pete giggled, wiping tears from his eyes. 'We can't just go barging back in there and ask her to hand over her pants.'

Binko thought for a moment, then his eyes lit up. 'You'll have to get into

trouble again.' He smiled brightly.

'Genius!' cried Pete. 'That's it. If I cause enough chaos, I'll get sent back to Mrs Brimwell's office.'

'We have to get the pantpiper back before she leaves school,' Binko said urgently.

Pete nodded. 'Right. I'll get into trouble. That's it. I mean, how hard can that be?'

CHAPTER SIX

A PARP-FECT IDEA!

Getting into trouble was a lot harder than Pete thought.

Back in Miss Penicketty's class, Binko had slipped a drawing pin on to the teacher's chair. But the bell for break had rung before she'd sat down, and they were all sent out to play.

After break, a substitute teacher came in to teach an art lesson. Pete and Binko had flicked paint at the paper and made a mess

all over it. But rather than send him to the head, the art teacher had congratulated Pete on his 'amazing creativity', and let him off the rest of the lesson.

Even when Binko had designed a brilliant rice-pudding launcher and Pete splattered more than half the teachers and pupils in the canteen with sticky, lumpy goo, he hadn't been sent to the office.

Instead he'd been kept in at lunch break and told to write out 'I will not play with my food' a hundred times. The catapult he'd used for the launcher had been confiscated, too, along with his stink bombs, his itching powder, and the last few bits of mouldy pork pie in his pocket.

And now the day was over. The final bell had rung and Pete was shuffling out of the school building amongst the sea of pupils, headed towards the front gate.

'There's nothing more we can do,' he sighed. 'We can't follow her home. We'll just have to hope it's still there tomorrow.'

'Hmmm. Risky,' Binko told him. 'The more bum gas that thing gobbles, the more powerful it'll become. If we don't catch it soon, we may not be able to catch it at all.'

Pete wandered over to where G-Bob and Ollie usually waited for him. A group of older girls were gathered around Ollie, cooing at him. They were ignoring G-Bob, who was scratching his hairy ears.

'Awww, he's so cute!' one of the girls chirped.

'Me so coot,' Ollie agreed, flashing them a big smile.

G-Bob grinned too, revealing yellow, stained teeth and huge gummy spaces where some had rotted away completely.

Half-chewed lumps of sausage plugged the gaps, along with blobs of the gherkins and custard that he'd had for lunch.

The girls screamed in terror, then turned and raced away. G-Bob cackled loudly.

'G-Bob's recovered from eating the chilli then,' Pete sighed, as he strolled over to join his grandad and little brother. Halfway there, he stopped.

'You said the pantpiper is drawn to the smelliest person in the room, right?'

Binko nodded. 'Right.'

'What if we brought it the smelliest person *in the world*?'

'It'd be on 'em quicker than you could say Flurblemunt Rylox,' Binko said.

The little alien's gaze fell on G-Bob, who was now licking sausage grease from his wiry beard. 'Oh,' Binko giggled. 'Right. How do we get him to the office, though?'

'Watch and learn,' Pete smiled. 'Hi, G-Bob. Hi, Ollie,' he called as he strolled over to them. 'G-Bob, can you come with me for a minute? I want to show you something that . . . Actually, no, it doesn't matter.'

G-Bob scowled. 'Wot?' he demanded. 'Show me wot?'

'Oh, no, nothing, nothing,' Pete said. 'Forget it. You wouldn't be interested.'

'I might. Tell me.'

'Naaah, it's just they're cleaning out the canteen. There's loads and loads of tins of out-of-date corned beef that they're just throwing away.'

Up by Pete's ear, Binko giggled.

'It's just sitting there out by the bins,' Pete continued. 'I dunno if you want to –'

'SHOW ME!' cried G-Bob.

'OK!' replied Pete, smiling broadly. He caught G-Bob by the arm, grabbed hold of Ollie, then led them quickly across the playground and back into the school.

Pete marched along until they reached Mrs Brimwell's door. 'It's just in here . . .' he said, knocking.

'G-go away! I'm not in,' whimpered Mrs Brimwell from inside her office.

Pete knocked again, then pushed the door open. The head teacher was still in her seat. Her hands were on her knees, holding her skirt in place. They were shaking slightly.

'Sorry, Mrs Brimwell,' Pete said, pulling G-Bob and Ollie into the room. 'I just wanted you to meet my grandad.'

'Now's not a good time,' Mrs Brimwell groaned, clutching her tummy. Her hair looked like an ostrich had tried to nest in it, and her glasses were wonky and steamed up. She was panting like a stream train.

'Where's this old beef then?' G-Bob demanded, pulling his arm free of Pete's grip. 'I know it's here somewhere, I can smell it.'

Mrs Brimwell frowned. 'B-beef?'

'This nose o' mine never lies,' G-Bob told her. He was stalking around the room, sniffing at the air. 'An' I can smell somethin' stinky. Meaty, yes, but eggy, too.' He took another sniff. 'An' a bit rotten.'

'An' pooey!' shouted Ollie, pinching his nose.

A movement down at the band of the head teacher's skirt caught Binko's eye. There, barely visible, was the pantpiper's snout. 'It's working!' he whispered. 'It's picking up G-Bob's stink.'

'But look at Mrs Brimwell's face,' Pete replied, quietly. 'She looks like she's going to burst.'

‘You’re right,’ Binko said. He pressed a few buttons on his spacesuit and a countdown appeared. ‘By my calculations, she’s going to drop an absolute whopper in three . . . two . . . one . . .’

There was a tiny squeal, like the air being released from a balloon. A flicker of relief passed across Mrs Brimwell’s face, but it didn’t last long.

A split-second later . . .

BOOM!

A sound like a ship's foghorn filled the room. The force of the pantpiper's gas-blast knocked Ollie off his feet and blew Mrs Brimwell's skirt out like an open parachute. For a brief moment, Pete caught a flash of long frilly red pants, before the skirt drifted gently back down into place.

G-Bob stood still, his mouth hanging open. Then the corners of his mouth slowly curved upwards into a smile, as the whiff from the pantpiper's mega-trump wafted towards him.

'Mmmmm,' he muttered, inhaling deeply. 'Sumfing smells good.'

Pete stuffed his tie into his mouth to stop himself laughing.

'There, look. Under the desk!' Binko cried.

Pete looked down and spotted the pantpiper, scurrying across the carpet.

It bounced along on its stubby legs, its eye stalks swivelling around like periscopes. It snuffled over to G-Bob's shoe, then scampered straight up the old

man's wrinkled trouser leg.

'Here goes nothing,' Binko said, hurrying down Pete's arm. He leaped on to G-Bob's back, then disappeared down the back of his grubby, holey trousers.

Pete waited anxiously for Binko to reappear. Mrs Brimwell was leaning back in her chair, looking dazed but relieved. G-Bob scratched his bum, but it didn't seem like he had noticed the tussle in his trouser leg. Finally a little hand caught hold of the grubby length of string G-Bob used as a belt, and Binko pulled himself free, dragging the ickimal with him. His face looked even greener than usual.

Pete quickly snatched Binko and the pantpiper from the back of G-Bob's trousers and dropped them carefully into his own trouser pocket. 'Right, time to go,' he announced, grabbing G-Bob by the arm. Stopping to pick up Ollie, Pete hurried out of the room, leaving a very confused Mrs Brimwell behind.

G-Bob grinned, forgetting all about

the corned beef. 'Now *that*,' he said, pointing a bony finger back towards Mrs Brimwell's office door, 'is what I call a woman!'

Later that evening, Pete stood in his bedroom, looking down at the bloated ickimal in his hand. It lay on its back, its

bulging belly pointing up at the ceiling.

'What are we going to do with it?' he wondered. 'We can't keep it in my room. It smells bad enough in here as it is.'

'What we need,' answered Binko, 'is somewhere that's already really smelly.'

Pete looked out of the window. Just then Willow wandered down the garden carrying a bucket full of gunky vegetables from the freezer. She threw them on the compost heap by G-Bob's shed.

She'd started it years ago, and had been adding kitchen scraps and other rubbish to it ever since. Every time Pete passed it, he had to hold his breath so that the fumes didn't burn his throat.

It was *perfect.*

Pete raced downstairs and hurried out to the rotting pile. By the time he was halfway there, the pantpiper was on its feet. By the time they reached the compost heap, it had started bouncing up and down excitedly.

'Now he'll be safe until we've caught the rest,' Pete said, lowering the ickimal on to the heap. It rolled around, drinking in the stink and snuffling loudly. 'And no one will notice a few more smelly gases here.'

Pete ran back up to his room and had a celebratory jump on his bed, with Binko

clinging on to his hair as it flapped up and down. After three triumphant star jumps in a row Pete flopped backwards and Binko curled into his belly button.

'So, that's two ickimals captured,'

Binko sighed happily. 'The Intergalactic Duo have done it again!'

'And the next one will be easier,' Pete said, putting his arms behind his head. 'I mean, it can't be hiding anywhere worse than Mrs Brimwell's pants.'

Binko giggled. 'Do you know something?' he said with a huge yawn. 'I've got a funny feeling you're going to wish you hadn't said that.'

THE END

THE PANTPIPER